Contents

Nick

Nick's older brother Ben

Kylie's friend Claire

Nick's twin sister Kylie

Nick's got a problem.

Well, two problems:

1

He fancies Claire. Claire acts like he
doesn't exist.

2

He's not popular with big, bad Barry Budgen –
and when Barry doesn't like you, he makes
sure you know about it!

Barry
Budgen

How can Nick get rid of Barry once and for all,
and make Claire notice him?

Sounds impossible?
Maybe, but Nick has a cunning plan ...

Chapter 1

I don't understand girls.

And my brother Ben doesn't either.

It's much worse for Ben, of course. He's six years older than me, so girls are a real big problem for him.

They never used to be a problem for me at all. Not until I met Claire.

It's not like I fancy her or anything.

But that's not the problem. The problem is, she hates me.

How do I know?

Why else would she get up and move every time I sit down near her at break?

Why else would she tell Kylie to tell me to stop hanging around them all the time?

Kylie is my twin sister. She's also Claire's best friend.

I know, it was a dumb question. But like Ben says, there's two things that'll make a lad go stupid every time. One is money, the other is girls.

Ben's always giving me advice, whether I ask for it or not.

He told me I should be 'cool'.

Girls don't like it if you're not cool.

I didn't know what he meant. So he told me.

"It isn't cool to hang around all the time and let them know you fancy them."

I sat down on a rock and scratched my ear.

I didn't say I fancy her.

No, that's why you suddenly started hanging around Kylie again. You didn't even do that in primary school.

He was right, as usual. Kylie and me are twins, but we don't do too much together. She's always been such a … girl.

Well, Ben might be older than me, but he didn't have any answers. Claire still hated me.

Then, suddenly, it didn't matter.
Two things happened that *did* matter, and I forgot all about girls.

I was much too busy trying to work out a way to stay alive!

Chapter 2

Two things happened, and they both had to do with Barry Budgen. Big, bad Barry Budgen.

You know what kids are like. Budgen ... Budgie. Nicknames are funny things.

I wish I could say *he* was funny, but he was about as funny as an axe-murderer.

And twice as ugly. Everyone called him 'Budgie' behind his back, but you had to be brave – or stupid – to call him anything like that to his face.

I like budgies. They're small and cute.
I didn't like Barry. He was big and mean. And
he had plans to kill me.

It all started off like one of those old
jokes.

*I've got some good news and I've got
some bad news ...*

The good news was that I made the school
football team.

The bad news was that Bad Barry Budgen
didn't. And that he blamed me because I did.

And because he blamed me, he made sure
I knew what I was 'in for'.

I nearly asked the question, but I didn't.

It's hard to be a smart ... alec, when the guy you want to be a smart alec to is twice as big as you and twice as ugly as an axe-murderer.

And it's *really* hard to be a smart *anything* if he has two fistfuls of the front of your shirt and has you lifted up off the ground.

Not high. He just lifted me up so that my face was level with his. Which meant my feet were hanging just about two inches above the footpath.

I don't know why he blamed me.
There were twelve other kids on the team, so why me?

I guess it was because I was the substitute. Have you ever seen me play football? Ben always reckoned Kylie would make a better full-back.

Which might tell you just how bad Barry Budgen was.

But I guess he didn't see it that way. If you could call what went on inside his head *thinking,* he probably thought I'd creeped to the coach, or something.

He probably also thought that if he could scare me out of playing, they'd need another player, and he would get a go.

Maybe he would have, but with his skill, I think that the coach would more likely pick Kylie …

And we were never going to find out, because he wasn't going to scare me out of playing.

I wasn't going to let him.

I'm not a hero, but I never got picked for any team before and I wasn't going to give it up.

I guess I forgot just how big Barry was. And just how mean ...

It started off with little things.

He'd steal my bag and hide it in the girls' toilet.

Don't ask me how he got it in there. I didn't ask him. I guess even *he* has friends. Or kids he can scare into doing anything.

I had to tell Mr Smythe that I didn't know how it kept ending up in there. If I'd told him the truth, he would probably have believed me, but I was in enough trouble with Barry already.

So, I kept quiet.
And he kept on …

1 He let down the tyres on my bike ...

2 and took my pump ...

3 ... so I couldn't ride home.

22

4 The next day, he put a second padlock on my chain, so I couldn't even take my bike out of the bike shed.

5 I had to get a saw and cut the chain.

6 He even put sugar all through my bag ...

7 and left it on an ants' nest.

24

It took me half an hour to find the bag. I didn't mind that very much because I missed out on half an hour of Maths. But when I found it, it was full of tiny crawling things. Which I *did* mind.

Really, they weren't so tiny. They were big ants, and when I picked the bag up, one bit me.

It took ages to get them out of my bag and my books and my pencil case.

And my lunch was ruined. Some things
you just don't want on your sandwiches!

Not that I got to eat my lunch any more.
He started taking that too.

Every day.

That was when I got my big idea . . .

Chapter 3

As well as not being too good at football, Barry isn't too bright either. Ben reckons Barry's nickname suits him; he's about as smart as a budgie.

I got a book for Christmas which told you how to do all sorts of dumb stuff that you wouldn't want to do anyway.

But some of the things were funny.

Like how to make a chicken go to sleep.

It's easy to hypnotise a chicken, or so the book said. So I thought, maybe it's easy to hypnotise a budgie too!

Or at least it might be easy to make him think I could.

It was such a simple plan.

All I had to do was let him take my lunch.

OK, so it doesn't sound like such a great plan. Especially when I was facing certain death at the hands of the Classmate from Hell. But hear me out. It gets better.

Anyway, death isn't so bad. My gran told me that. She's 88 and she lives with us. She's not scared of dying. She just doesn't like being old.

MY GRAN

She has to take pills to sleep and pills to wake up. And she has to eat this special laxative chocolate to help her ... you know. To help her go to the toilet.

Look, I'll tell you about Gran another time. Now where was I? That's right, the plan ...

The lunch was the key. Two cheese sandwiches, a piece of home-made chocolate cake and half a bar of chocolate.

I made the cake myself the night before. But I didn't use ordinary chocolate; not for this cake. I used my gran's special chocolate. And the half a bar was what was left over after I'd made the cake.

There must have been two weeks' worth of that chocolate in my lunch-box when Barry got to it.

He ate the lot – like always.

Then, just before the end of lunch, I walked up to him. I made sure there was a teacher close enough to see us.

Just in case things went wrong.

"Budgie," I said. He really hated people calling him that. Still, I had to get him mad if the plan was going to work.

I don't want you to take my lunch any more. I've let you up 'til now, because I didn't want to use my powers. But that's it.

He just looked at me. A bit like an ape might look at one of its fleas.

Just before the flea got squashed.

He knew I couldn't do that. *His* big
brother was bigger than mine!

It was my turn to just look at him.

"I don't need to."

Then I did it. I looked right into his eyes. I
held my hand out so that all the fingers
pointed at his face.

And I said something.

I don't remember what I said. It doesn't
matter. The word didn't mean anything.

"Have you gone mad?"

It was a good question. There were lots of
kids around and they were all watching. He'd
have to beat me up. That's basic bully law.
Everyone knows it.

Maybe I *was* mad.

But it was too late to go back.

"I don't need anyone. You see, I just hypnotised you. From now on, any time you think about hitting me ... "

I stopped talking, and looked at the kids around us. Then I went on ...

39

I stepped out where Mr Smythe could see me. Just in case.

"If you don't believe me, I'll be waiting by the back gate after school," I said, then I smiled at Claire.

She was standing there with the others.

She didn't smile back, but she didn't look at me like I was a worm either.

Things were looking up already.

Chapter 4

I won't say I wasn't scared. I *was*. But it was the best plan I could think of.

And at least it made people notice me. Even if Barry was going to kill me.

By the end of school I knew it was working. Twice that afternoon Barry had to go to the toilets. And he was looking really worried when he came to the back gate at 3.15.

"How are you feeling?" I asked him. And I smiled. Claire was there again. So were half the school.

He didn't say anything. But he was moving from foot to foot and crossing his legs.

Then he was running. Back towards the toilets.

He didn't make it.

You could tell by the way he slowed down
and began to walk funny.

I wouldn't have to. He wasn't going to
give me any more trouble.

Chapter 5

When I got home, Gran was at it already.

I knew what she was talking about, but I asked anyway.

What did you lose, Gran?

Maybe I didn't get them after all. I do hope my memory isn't going. I don't usually forget things . . .

She wasn't talking to me, really. She was worried.

I felt bad.

"Anything I can do?" I asked.

She looked at me.

"Nicky," she said. She always called me that, since I was a baby.

"Nicky, I need some of my special chocolates. You know. The ones that help me ... "

She didn't like to talk about it.

So I said, "I'll go get some for you."

Like I said, I felt bad. I mean, I didn't want her to get sick, or anything.

You can get to feeling pretty bad if you can't ... you know ... go.

Chapter 6

Things are going great at school.
Barry stays out of my way. And I get to eat
my lunch in peace.

I'm still on the football team. And Barry isn't.

I think I said before, I'm not a hero. But I'm a lot more popular than I was a few weeks ago.

And best of all, Claire lets me hang
around. Even when Kylie isn't there. She even
comes to sit next to me, sometimes …

So, yeah. Things are looking up.

TEEN LIFE, SET C

Crush *by Jon Blake*

Ian's class have a wild time with their media studies project ... Somehow that video camera seems to land everyone in trouble – especially Ian!

Sweet Revenge *by Brian Caswell*

Nick's got a problem. He's being picked on by Budgie the bully – and he's had enough! He comes up with a plan to have a very sweet revenge.

Love from Katy *by Jacqueline Wilson*

Katy really likes Dave, a boy she's met on the bus. She doesn't dare tell him how she feels. So she writes letters instead – letters she never means to send. What would happen if Dave saw her letters?

Darryl

TEEN LIFE, SET D

Darryl seems so perfect. But he stays out of trouble by making Paul take the blame – and Paul won't be pushed around for ever!

IF YOU LIKED **SWEET REVENGE**,
YOU MIGHT ENJOY ...

Hall End High
Books 1 to 4

by Mary Hooper

TEEN LIFE, SET B

Miss Hogan wants to give Year 8 at Hall End High a test.

Gary, Jenny, Ray and Carly want to stop her!

The four friends take it in turns to think up a brilliant hoax to stop the test. Gary goes first. Then Jenny, Ray and Carly have a go. Can they stop Miss Hogan? One thing's for sure – they have fun trying!

ANOTHER BOOK YOU MIGHT ENJOY ...

My Secret Love
by Andy Brown

by Narinder Dhami

TEEN LIFE, SET D

"I've been in love now since 8.43 a.m. on January 14th, and it feels GREAT."

Andy loves Beth. But how can he tell her? Whenever he sees her, something's bound to go wrong ...

ANOTHER BOOK YOU MIGHT ENJOY ...

Escape from the Rave Police

by Jon Blake

HUMOUR, SET C

It's 2079, and if you don't like to dance, you'd better look out. With the Rave Police about, there's no escape from the party ...

ANOTHER BOOK YOU MIGHT ENJOY ...

Demons in Disguise

by Jean Ure

HUMOUR, SET C

Steven is just about to start his first teaching job. He thinks the boys at the posh school will be well-behaved and polite.

He is in for a nasty surprise!